A Present From Lulu

Caroline Uff

ORCHARD BOOKS

A Present From Lulu

To Maddy and Bea
with love from me

ORCHARD BOOKS
338 Euston Road, London NW1 3BH
Orchard Books Australia
Level 17/207 Kent Street, Sydney, NSW 2000

First published in 2009 by Orchard Books
First published in paperback in 2010
ISBN 978 1 84362 616 9
Text and illustrations © Caroline Uff 2009

1 3 5 7 9 10 8 6 4 2

Printed in China

Orchard Books is a division of Hachette Children's Books, an Hachette UK company.
www.hachette.co.uk

Today, Lulu and Granny are shopping for the perfect present for Mummy.

Lulu thinks very hard . . . What would Mummy really like?

Up, up, up they go
on the escalator.
Hold on tight,
Lulu!

Lulu loves the
cuddly lion,

but it's not quite
right for Mummy.

What about a book?
Mummy loves reading.

Granny and Lulu
do too.

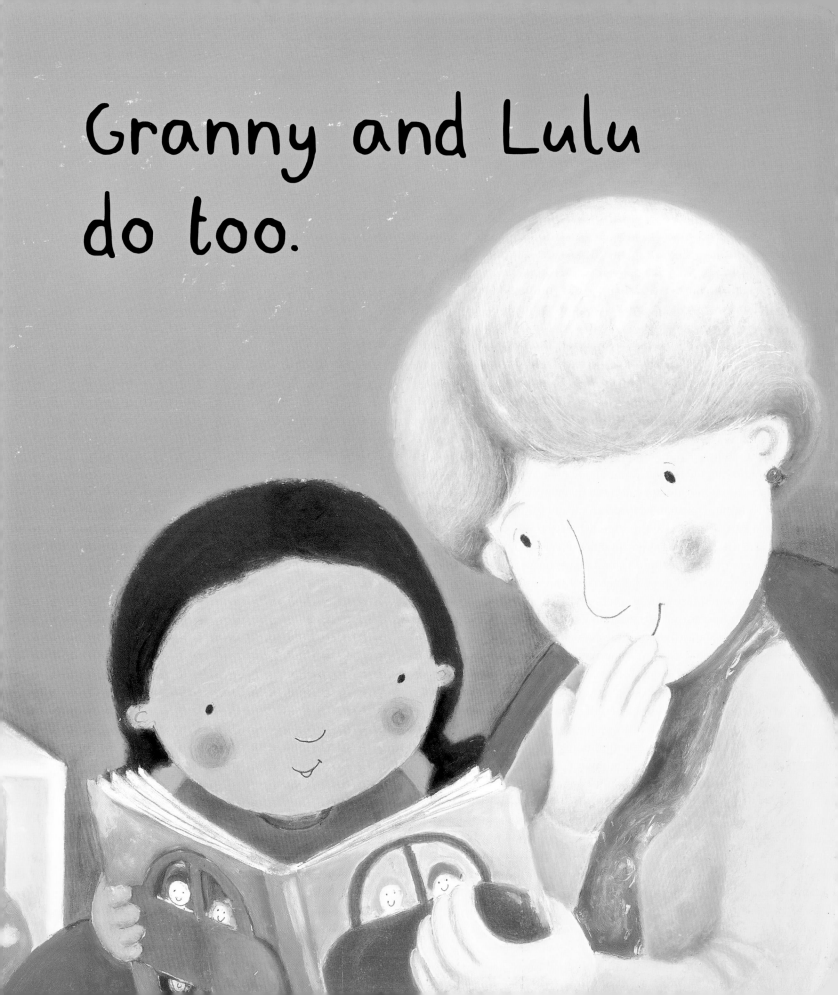

Maybe Mummy would like some yummy chocolates,

or a pink sugar mouse?

Perhaps a candle
that smells just
like roses?

Or a pretty,
floaty scarf?

Would Mummy like some sunglasses, just like a film star?

Oh, look! A sparkly necklace – perfect for Mummy!

It's time to go. Granny buys the book and candle. Lulu buys the necklace for Mummy.

Mummy loves
her necklace.
"Thank you, Lulu!
What a perfect
present!"